BLUFF YOUR WAY IN
BRITISH THEATRE

Fidelis Morgan

CENTENNIAL PRESS

ISBN 0-8220-2203-6
U.S. edition © Copyright 1989 by Centennial Press
British edition © Copyright 1986 by The Bluffer's Guides

Printed in U.S.A.

Centennial Press, Box 82087, Lincoln, Nebraska 68501
an imprint of Cliffs Notes, Inc.

INTRODUCTION

In theatrical matters, a bluffer's life is a dicey business. While the average bus driver would not feel compelled to advise a brain surgeon which scapel to use, nor would a hairdresser be driven to criticize the choice of valves made by an electrical engineer, when it comes to the theatre, every Tom, Dick, and Harry has his own analysis of where the writer, director, and actors went wrong. On top of this there are hundreds of people who have spent 40 years or more locked in a library becoming specialists in Grand Guignol acting in Serbo-Croatia between 1857 and 1859.

There is absolutely no point in attempting to learn by rote a list of world dramatists from 1000 B.C. to today, together with the names of all their plays, because you are sure to recount the amazing life stories of the women playwrights of the Restoration to someone who has just written a book about them.

When surrounded by so many experts of varying degree, the only advice we can offer is the old adage "If you've got a humpback put a frill round it" (make them jealous of your ignorance by passing it off as freshness and originality).

On the other hand, there is no point looking an absolute fool. The theatre, like any business, is packed with jargon designed to exclude the uninitiated. You do not want to spend the best part of a discussion on the problems facing Equity wondering why actors should get so heated about what's going on in the Stock Exchange. Nor when an actor greets you with, "I'm giving a salad in the park!" do you want to labor under the misapprehension that you have been invited to a picnic.

You do not need to know everything about world theatre from the Fol de Rols to Fuerte Ovejuna. You simply need enough facts to get you by.

Don't forget to apply any knowledge at all to get the conversation where you want it. For example, when someone tries to impress you by saying that they're off to the Pitlochry Festival Theatre, simply tell them that Pitlochry is the birthplace of Pontius Pilate (son of one of the Romans in Britain), and you've steered them away from any discussion of plays you've never heard of.

And never forget you're not the only bluffer. In the world of theatre *everybody* is one. Actors who talk of having "something in the pipeline" are simply out of work; directors who discuss their new "interpretation" are describing a production everyone else thought of years ago and dismissed as nonsense, and so it goes on and on.

The most important weapon you have is your own confidence in the fact that you know practically nothing and your determination to keep it that way.

Theatre People

The actors' trade union, **Equity**, manages to get into the national news twice a year: once to announce that the entire population of Albania, Nepal, Upper Volta, and Swaziland added together is less than the total number of British actors without a job, and later in the year to claim that they are fighting off more leftwing takeover bids than the Labor Party. Apart from that they don't do much.

Equity's membership is composed of actors, directors, designers, opera singers, stage managers, and both ballet and belly dancers.

The actor Michael Wilding once said that you can recognize **actors** by the glazed look that comes into their eyes when the conversation wanders away from themselves. They also seem to talk 700 decibels louder than the average man in the street.

Directors are far more chameleonlike. *Bad directors* often wear leather jackets and Cuban-heeled boots and speak when they're not spoken to. They give the actor such helpful advice as "Follow the thrust of the subtext and the momentum of your given circumstances, and let the units' impetus mark the rhythm of the dynamic." And the actor in deep trouble may be comforted with the note "Your explorations are uncontained." *Good directors*, a much rarer breed, can be recognized only by an intelligent twinkle in the eye.

In the world of opera and ballet, **tenors** are fat, **basses** are tall, **ballerinas** are practically midgets, and for all the others, your guess is as good as ours.

Auditions

Each production that you see begins its working life with **auditions.** These are generally held in a theatre, usually onstage on someone else's set. So a potential King Henry V can find himself summoning the troops to battle in the oak-beamed, chintzy front room of the Vicarage at Little Muckton-under-Ouse. The actor stands in a blast of light on the stage while the director sits smugly in the stalls shouting, "Thank you *so* much . . . Next!" Sometimes auditions are held in dusty church halls and, if you are very unlucky, in seedy West London hotel rooms.

There are two principal ways actors discover where and when a certain audition is to take place:

(1) The artist's **agent** (a person who takes between 5 and 15 percent of the actor's wages and 100 percent of the blame for anything that the actor is miserable about) arranges an audition on his or her client's behalf.

(2) The artist hears about it on the **grapevine,** which is an unsavory method of picking up as much information as possible from friends who failed to get the job yesterday or who are eagerly awaiting a **recall** for tomorrow.

It is rumored that some actors read about auditions in *The Stage,* the so-called organ of the theatrical profession. In any week, one might expect to find 53 advertisements for topless waitresses in Beirut and one for the production of *Godspell* which closed last Saturday.

Some actors, of course, no longer have to audition and are merely phoned and offered the part. These are usually the actors whose names appear above the title on the poster for the show in question.

There are various job descriptions for the work (**parts** or **roles**) available: The **lead,** is what most people seem to play (or **give**). It is not uncommon to meet twelve actors, all with different parts in the same production, every one of whom claims to be playing the lead. Never question this claim or you might have to listen to a diatribe about how the play may be **called** *Hamlet*, but in fact it is the role of Osric that makes or breaks it.

Actors who can actually admit that they are not the lead describe their parts as

(1) a cameo
(2) small, but meaningful
(3) a spit and a cough
(4) bread-and-butter work

These honest folk generally describe themselves as jobbing or middle-range actors. They often wear reefer jackets, paisley scarves, twill trousers, and Hush Puppies. Men and women alike.

A couple of smallish parts are specifically described as **the salads** — Salerio and Solanio in *The Merchant of Venice.* Hence, "I'm giving a salad in the park" translates as "I'm playing Salerio or Solanio at the Open Air Theatre, Regents Park."

Early in most actors' careers, they will be expected to take nonspeaking roles known as **walk-ons, extras,** and **supers.** They might also **understudy,** or **cover,** one of the leads. If they're unlucky.

Venues

All of these parts will be played in one of the following theatres:

The West End — which includes all of the older style theatres in Central London, where productions are generally funded by production companies backed by **angels,** rich fools with money to throw down the drain.

The National or **The RSC**—publicly funded labyrinthine buildings with no windows and nylon carpets which give off more static electricity than Battersea Power Station.

The Fringe—drafty basements, attics, and rooms above pubs with little money, where general bonhomie and artistic ardor are supposed to compensate for the miserable lack of comfort.

A Number One Tour—a leftover from the days when there were hundreds of touring theatres which were rated on a sliding scale similar to that of the Michelin guides. Nowadays, whether the tour visits Edwardian theatres, civic buildings, or school sports halls, no one ever admits to being less than a number one tour.

Rep—Regional, generally publicly funded, theatres. There is a strict hierarchy of reps, which is subject to sudden and unaccountable change. The acquisition of a job at Barrow-in-Furness Rep might inspire gasps of admiration on a Monday, but if you mention it the following Wednesday, you will find yourself being shunned at parties and refused a table at Joe Allen's.

Rehearsals

Rehearsals take about four weeks, although current fashion allows anything up to six months. Once rehearsals were adequately described by the French word for them — *répétitions*. But lately, a tendency has developed to hold **organic** rehearsals, which swing between nursery-school-type game playing and dry, academic discussions of the influences of post-Freudian floccinaucinihilipilification of the play in hand.

The first rehearsal usually begins with a **read-through,** where the play is read through. In the old days, this task fell to the playwright, whose standards of reading must have so appalled the members of the cast and director that they now do it themselves. The actors sit in a semicircle and mumble and mutter their way slowly through the piece. The few actors who shout and read with much bravado on these occasions can generally be depended upon to give the worst performances in the finished production.

It is worth noting that some actors use the read-through as a chance to weigh up the potential bedability quotient of the rest of the cast. When not speaking, these actors can be found scanning the bodies of the people they fancy and giving them points out of ten.

The director sits at one end of the rehearsal room behind a desk littered with dirty coffee cups, chewed dog-ends of (usually French) cigarettes, screwed up pieces of paper, and mangled copies of the **script.** Next to him/her sits (if the theatre is rich enough to have one) the **assistant director** and the **assistant stage manager** (**ASM**), whose job it is to write down the actors' moves as they are set, or **blocked.**

Some directors (and these are almost always actors manqués) insist on getting up every two seconds, rushing out onto the acting area, and giving the actor what is meant to be the definitive reading of a line. At these moments it takes all the self-control the actor has not to burst into derisive laughter. However, actors with a bit of experience have learned to nod seriously, hold their chin in one hand, say with a tone of dawning enlightenment, "Aaaaaaaaaah I seeeeeeee!" and then continue doing exactly what they were doing before.

Actors who are not in the scene being rehearsed can generally be found in the nearest pub, where they claim to be learning their lines. Actors who are in the scene, but not the particular bit of it that is being rehearsed, huddle around the edge of the room on uncomfortable benches and folding chairs. The least intelligent make a big show of doing the *Times* or *Guardian* crossword (the *Guardian* is a compulsory part of an actor's uniform); some actresses bring their knitting or tatting or sewing or macramé, but this style of rehearsal time-filling is no longer a female prerogative. Some actors make a big show of modesty while chuckling over the fan mail which arrived with the morning's mail and which they posted to themselves the day before. Fired by the electric atmosphere of the rehearsal room, others sleep.

Toward the end of the rehearsal period, actors experience the runs:

Word runs—Where the actors, without doing any of the moves, speak through the play as though for radio.

Speed runs—Where the actors perform the play as though it is an LP being played at 45 rpm. Some actors are marvelous at this; others just go on doing it as they always have done it. When the speed runs are taken at a real lick, they are exhilarating and hilarious for all.

Dry runs – More easily explained in relation to opera productions where the singers sing every note accurately but make no effort to "sing out," doing the musical equivalent to mumbling. For actors it is the same; instead of playing out, the whole thing is done for accuracy of words and moves and not for strength of acting.

The rehearsal period comes to a ghastly climax with the technical rehearsal (the **tec**), which is usually a stop-start rehearsal lasting all day and into the early hours of the morning after, during the course of which the set designer discovers that none of the dresses fit through the doors; the lighting designer realizes that the lighting plot overloads the system and causes blackouts throughout a five-mile radius of the theatre; the stage management is finally made to understand that when the director asked for the back wall of the stable scene to be covered in yokes, he had not said yolks; the director sends the assistant director out to buy Valium, and the actors, not used to being ignored, try to regain attention by making up new lines, coming on with their flies undone and their wigs on back-to-front, falling off the edge of the stage and breaking their ankles, or collapsing in the wings and being rushed to hospital where tests confirm that they are suffering from a little-known condition called everyone-forgot-me-during-the-tec syndrome.

The final, or dress, rehearsal (the **dress**) is a much more somber affair. It is usually conducted exactly as a public performance would be (no stopping if anything goes wrong), and the stage manager times it with a stopwatch. This is the moment when the actors, through a miasma of fear, begin to realize what they've let themselves in for. Meanwhile, everyone else in the building, now beyond terror, starts making remarks like "worse things happen at sea" and "que sera sera!" Some even trot out the old and utterly fallacious adage "bad dress; good show." By this time the director has mentally left the production and has started working on his or her next.

Performance

The **first night,** a social occasion providing much the same pleasures as the rattle of the tumbrils and the swish of the guillotine, is attended by

(1) **Critics** (the Mesdames Defarge of the audience).
(2) **Friends of the cast** (a raggle-taggle band of aristocrats in disguise), mumbling prayers of relief that they're not on the other side of the curtain.
(3) A group of self-styled **culture vultures** determined to have as vile an evening as possible (the mob).

As a result the first-night audience is entirely different from any other, and the noises coming from it can be broken down as follows:

(1) From the critics, a black and ominous silence. This does not necessarily indicate that they're not enjoying themselves thoroughly. It is their feeble attempt to prevent the other critics from knowing what they actually think.
(2) From the friends, hopelessly misguided support in the form of screams of delight at each tired joke, occasional attempts to lead the audience

into entirely unspontaneous applause after each character enters or exits, and cat-calls and wolf-whistles at the end.

(3) From the culture vultures, the eternal rustling of programs and candy wrappers.

Afterward there is a frantic rush backstage to congratulate the actors, however bad they might have been. The point is, you see, that they got through it and didn't take a flight to Papua New Guinea during the interval.

Backstage

One can sometimes get past the **stage-door man** with a breezy familiarity: "Hello there, Fred. Hope you're keeping well! What number's Miss X?" But the stage-door man is on the whole a very hard nut to crack. Most of them are well weathered against bluffers, even those with £5 notes hidden in the palms of their hands. The best bet for anyone with a built-in compass is to attempt the **pass door,** a door marked "Private" which links the auditorium to the backstage area. But this strategem can be lethal because backstage every theatre is indistinguishable from the Hampton Court Maze.

Presuming you have made your way into the inner sanctum, or **dressing room** (where the offending actors sit surrounded by good-luck telegrams, greasy wigs on hat stands, and disgusting stumps of makeup strewn over a counter covered with a small hand towel or doily), you then encounter a whole new language and many strange customs, which must be observed if you are not to seem the leprous outsider that you obviously are.

First, take it as read that you will be addressed as "darling." This is partly meant in affection and partly because the actors haven't a clue who you are, even if you are their husband or wife. The adrenalin of the evening's performance and the relief that it's over are so overwhelming that your name is literally irrelevant.

As a member of the audience, you have been one of the **punters,** or **bums on seats.** Perhaps you sat in the gallery, or **gods,** or in the back of the gallery, or **woods.** Perhaps you were lucky enough to get a free ticket, or **comp.** Perhaps most of the audience did, in which case it was a **papered house.**

All play titles will be abbreviated, usually to one word — for instance, *The Merchant of Venice* becomes Merchant, *A Midsummer Night's Dream* becomes The Dream, and *Look Back in Anger* becomes Anger. There are a few exceptions; *Nicholas Nickleby* is Nick-Nick, *Les Misérables* is The Glums, and the adaptation of *À La Recherche du Temps Perdu* called *A Waste of Time* is The Proust.

Tabs — Curtains.

Wings — Offstage sides of the stage.

Pros (pronounced *pross*) — Proscenium arch.

Cyc (pronounced *syke*) — Cyclorama, or tight screenlike curtain round the back of the stage.

Flies — Area above the stage where pieces of scenery are "flown."

Traps — Holes in the stage through which actors can emerge as though from the bowels of the earth.

Iron – The safety curtain.

Flats – Areas of canvas, stretched on wood and painted, which make up the walls of the set.

Floats – Footlights (now rarely used except in pantomime).

Green room – A rat infested hole where actors relax.

Some simple but essential elements of performance jargon are

Perf – Performance.

To dry – To forget one's words.

To fluff – To mess up one's words.

Corpse – Unrehearsed fit of uncontrollable laughter.

Props – Properties, items on stage.

Business – Overacting with a prop, usually a soda siphon.

Pracs – Props which actually work, like lighters and soda siphons.

Rounds – Spontaneous bursts of applause usually on an actor's entrance or exit or at the end of a song or dance.

Cue – The line after which an actor enters or has to speak his or her own line.

Doobries – Anything you've forgotten the name of.

Slap – Makeup.

The curtain, or **call** – Lineup of actors at the end of each performance.

Your call—Time at which each individual actor is expected to be in the theatre or the rehearsal room—for example, "What time is my call tomorrow?"

The run—Length of time during which a play is performing at a theatre, not to be confused with the *runs* (see *Rehearsals*)

Then there are the time calls, which are all five minutes fast, since this is supposed to be the length of time it takes an actor to get from the dressing room to the stage:

The half—The time all actors have to be in the building, thirty-five minutes before curtain up.

The quarter—Twenty-minute warning before the show.

The five—Ten-minute warning.

Beginners—Call to the stage for the actors who appear in the opening scene, five minutes before curtain up.

Many theatrical expressions take the form of directions—off, up, in, out, etc., and these must not be confused:

To go up—To begin the performance; also to corpse.

To come down—To finish the performance.

The walk down—Parade of grinning actors in ascending order of importance at the end of a show, culminating in the curtain (usually only in pantomimes and musicals).

To go in—To start a West End run.

To come in—As above.

The get in (also known as the **fit-up**)—Time allocated to putting up the set. The opposite of which is not the *get out,* but the **strike.**

To be off—To fail to arrive onstage on your cue.

To be off the book—To have learned your lines.

To be on the book (usually in the form *still* on the book)—Not to have learned your lines.

Now for a few tricks of the trade:

Under-dressing—Method of putting on street clothes underneath the costume, usually for the curtain, so that the actor can make a quick getaway to the pub.

Upstaging—Method of taking a step upstage (stage floors usually slope toward the audience) so that the actor to whom the offending actor is talking has to play his line with his back to the audience.

Rhubarb—Contrary to popular belief, when actors huddle in groups for crowd scenes, or as decorative smatterings of characters around the stage, they do not say, "Rhubarb, Rhubarb, Rhubarb." Occasionally, someone trying to be frightfully witty might utter this word just to show that he would never dream of really using it. The odd method actor will turn up in a crowd scene in character saying things like "Ods bodkins, Mercutio, regard the disarray of yon Romeo's viridian hosiery"; most actors, however, would be mumbling, "Stewart's tights are falling down" or other topical remarks.

Last matinee pranks—Often during the last matinee, the actors play little jokes on each other with the intention of corpsing everyone else. All too often the joker finds the joke more hilarious than the others do. These jokes include filling the bottles of colored water and cold tea with real alcohol, dropping plastic dogdirts around the set, swapping costumes with another character, coming on in plastic tartan rain-hats, changing lines – for example, instead of "Would you like a cup of tea?" it will be "Would you like some haddock mousse?" etc.

Hidden scripts – Quite often an actor finds himself on opening night with the lines not quite learned. These occasions lead to desperate measures. Pages of script are hastily taped to the backs of pieces of furniture and onto props, lines are written in ball-point pen on the cuffs and the back of the hand, and extras can be spotted holding open scripts on their trays or behind their shields, ready to feed lines when necessary.

Now for some frequently used expressions relating to other actors:

See you on the green – See you onstage.

OTT – Over the top, said when an actor gives a part more energy than is entirely necessary. Since this expression has been swiped by other sectors of the community (Sloane Rangers, etc.), actors frequently do not speak the phrase at all but instead pull a face and at the same time with the right hand (palm downwards) make a horizontal sawing motion about six inches above their heads.

NAR – No acting required, initials seen scribbled in the

margin of a leading actor's script next to lines which do not demand any particular degreee of virtuosity.

Brave – Description given (in reverent tones) of a performance which the speaker found indescribably embarrassing.

Good value – Said of an actor whose performance, although of the most pitiful quality, is extremely noticeable.

He/she phoned his/her performance in – Said when an actor has apparently sleepwalked through the play.

He/she couldn't act his/her way out of a paper bag – Said of an actor who falls below a certain level of excellence.

He/she couldn't direct traffic – Said of a director who similarly falls below certain standards.

He/she couldn't direct pee into a bucket – As above.

Chorine – Chorus girl.

Actrine – Lesser actress.

Some of the lower orders of the acting profession have invented a whole new use of these theatrical expressions and refer to every experience of life as though it were a performance. This is quite possibly because otherwise they'd have so little opportunity to use the expressions at all.

The cult of life-as-a-performance is often demonstrated by adding the word *acting* to any phrase depicting a situation *outside* the theatre – for instance, standing at a bus stop acting, or doing a lot of biting my nails acting, or quietly trying to get on with eating my dinner acting. The effect is nauseatingly cloying and coy, but the relentless use of this figure of speech is hailed in some circles as wit.

It is just as well for playgoers to have a handful of stock phrases which can be used after any performance and which will get them out of having to express their opinion at all. This may seem an unnecessary move, but experience will show you that your real opinions will be pooh-poohed by anyone you are foolish enough to express them to. Far wiser to mutter quietly, "Have they never *heard* of Brecht?" or, "One sometimes longs for the return of Sir Johnston Forbes-Robertson." Useful also to lob the ball squarely into the other court, not by asking what everyone else thinks, which can only expose you as a vacillating fool, but by saying in outraged tones, "What *about* the second act!" Needless to say, great care should be taken in any remark made to the actors. Two fairly safe comments are "Isn't Ibsen (or whoever) a *wonderful* playwright" and "The director should be shot."

Do not disgrace yourself by using expressions which are used only by amateurs and ill-informed members of the public at large.

Do not ask how the actor learns all those lines, or wonder however they came up with that extraordinary makeup, or even worse, refer to "greasepaint."

Never describe an out-of-work actor as "resting," with or without a knowing look, or describe the profession of acting as "treading the boards."

Do not suggest that an actor who appears in straight plays is "legit." The only actors who are not legit are the ones who never knew their fathers.

Do not, whether you mean it or not, wish an actor

good luck, but instead shriek jovially, "Break a leg!"

And whatever you do, don't go blundering into the famous theatrical **superstitions** unless you want to find yourself being made to leave the room, turn three times in a counterclockwise direction, spit, swear, and finally beg readmission before being forgiven. Even if you are forgiven, you are unlikely to be asked back. Never quote from *Macbeth,* which is always referred to as "The Scottish Play," or by the more daring as "Maccers." It is difficult to know where to draw the line on quoting from this particular play. One might get away with saying, "God save the King" or "Knock, knock, who's there?" but would stand no chance whatsoever with "Double double, toil and trouble" or "Out damned spot." *Macbeth* has gained its unlucky reputation because most productions of it seem to be failures. This in turn is often blamed on the Bard himself, who is said to have used real black magic incantations for the witches' scenes.

A superstition which is based on a more practical consideration is whistling—or rather, not whistling. In the days before mechanization, the fly-men took their cues (to drop scenery and weights) from a complex system of whistles. So if you whistled in those days, the consequences could have been even worse than the abovementioned spitting ritual.

Another superstition, which luckily applies only to actors, is that they should never leave their soap in the dressing room or they will not work in that theatre again—a pretty good insurance policy in some cases, if only it were true. The fact behind the superstition is probably no more than the hastily fabricated self-justification of some penny-pinching Scrooge trying to explain the mysterious removal of an inch-long piece of scented slime from the wash basin during the final performance.

The breezy manner should be affected by the bluffer at all times. Performers should not be talked about with the reverential use of their whole names. For instance, never say, "Wasn't Timothy West marvelous!" but, "Timmy was good, wasn't he!" Abbreviated Christian names are the order of the day, but tread carefully, for some of these are not standard.

- Felicity – Foo – Kendal
- Rosalie – Bun – Crutchley
- Dinah – Mousse – Sheridan
- Elizabeth – Paddy – Larner
- Evelyn – Boo – Laye
- Michael – Bodger – Bogdanov
- Robert – Tim – Hardy

In all such special cases, use of the surname is essential. And just as one should always say Dame Peg or Sir John, there is one name which always comes with title, and this belongs to the unrivaled comedy actress Lovely-Judi-Dench.

When you are still in the dressing room, it might be suggested that you all "go for a bite at J's" (or J.A.'s). This suggestion is an invitation for supper at a theatrical restaurant which is famous for its late hours and its habit of giving your table (which you had booked over three months ago) to a minor television star and his mistress who have just popped in on the off-chance. Actors continue to go there in order to practice **rubbernecking** (scanning the other tables to see if there's anyone useful – like casting directors – to chat up) and **table-hopping** (deserting the friends they came with

26

so that they can sit with people who are more interesting, more famous, or more useful).

A POTTED HISTORY

Any would-be theatrical bluffer must have at least a sprinkling of facts from theatrical and dramatic history—so here they are.

The Greeks Had a Word for It

Theatre, drama, critic, comedian, scene, chorus, dialogue, tyrant, method, character, crisis, chaos, catastrophe—the most important words in the modern theatrical vocabulary come from ancient Greece.

The theatrical tradition evolved from the ancient **rites** of fertility and of Dionysus, the god of wine—rites which are still actively practiced by actors in the British regional repertory theatres.

Productions were paid for by a **choregus,** a wealthy citizen who was obliged to support the drama as part of his civic duty.

Theatres were built on hillsides and consisted of an **auditorium,** where the audience sat, **scena,** which made up the scenery, and an **orchestra,** where the actors stood. (The musicians had to sit on steps at the side of the stage.) The actors wore *chitons* (long shirts), masks, *cothurni* (high boots rather like the "wedgies" so fashionable in the early 1970s), and *onkos* (tall hats). Thus bedecked, looking like absolute fools, they performed classical comedies and tragedies.

The word **comedy** derives from *comos,* meaning

revel or *masquerade,* and with devastating Greek logic, the word **tragedy** comes from *tragos,* meaning *goat.*

No women were allowed to appear onstage, and in comedy, to make sure that the audience was left in no doubt which actors were meant to be women, the ones who weren't wore a **phallus,** a red leather penis of a size which would make Noel Coward sit up and take notice.

The most famous Greek actor was **Thespis,** who toured the provinces on the back of a cart. The expression "on the wagon" may have adequately described Thespis but can seldom be applied to his descendants, who, however, think it unendingly hilarious to refer to themselves as **thespians** (presumably because it is the only word in the English language which almost rhymes with *lesbian*). As a playwright, Thespis was the prizewinner in the Dionysian festival of 535 B.C.

The father of tragedy, **Aeschylus** (525–456 B.C.), was a soldier who fought at the battle of Marathon. He was responsible for the invention of **dialogue,** as his plays were the first to introduce two actors onstage at the same time, talking to each other. God only knows what plays were like before this brilliant innovation. He wrote 80 to 90 plays, but only seven of these have survived intact.

The fates of characters in Greek tragedies seem somewhat less outrageous when the deaths of their creators are investigated. Aeschylus himself died in Syracuse when an eagle, mistaking his bald head for a rock, dropped a tortoise on it.

Sophocles (496–406 B.C.), however, managed to live until he was 90, and of his 120 plays, 18 have won prizes, but only seven are extant. His plays have had much influence on later ages. Freud's complexes are named after Sophocles' characters, and Shelley had a volume of Sophocles' plays in his pocket when he drowned.

Euripides (484–406 B.C.), a recluse, managed to score a survival rate of 18 out of 92 plays but won only five prizes. In the tradition of Aeschylus, his end fitted his work, for in 408 B.C. he went to stay at the court of King Archelaus, whose dogs accidentally tore him to pieces.

So much for tragedy. The two principal comic writers were **Aristophanes** (448–380 B.C.), who wrote bawdy, topical, and sophisticated plays designated "old comedy," while the "new comedy" was provided by **Menander** (342–292 B.C.), who coined the phrase "Whom the gods love die young." Menander was a nephew of **Alexis** (another comic poet, no relation to Joan Collins).

When in Rome

Latin, the language of ancient Rome, provides us with more important theatrical words: *director, rehearsal, stage, conflict, actor, applause,* and *disaster.*

The Romans flew in the face of Aristotelian theory. They didn't want an imitation; they wanted the real thing. For the opening performance of the first permanent theatre, built by Pompey to seat 40,000 spectators, 500 lions and 200 elephants were killed. There were sea battles, water ballets, gladiatorial competitions, and chariot races. Prostitutes were hired so that the portrayal of sex would be more realistic, and the general tone slipped to that of contemporary television game shows. In this spirit, the audiences were showered not only with perfumed water but also with vouchers for money, groceries, holidays, and ultimately, modern apartments.

It was not surprising therefore that although **Seneca** (4 B.C.–65 A.D.) wrote at least a dozen plays, they were read only in private and were not performed in the theatres. Seneca was on nodding terms with all of the leading characters from *I Claudius:* Caligula tried to kill him, Messalina accused him of an intrigue with Julia and banished him to Corsica, and he eventually became tutor to Nero, who ordered him to commit suicide, which he did.

A great patron of the theatre, **Nero** was himself something of a playwright and actor. He would regularly star in all-day entertainments in theatres the size of the Roman Colosseum. The citizens of Rome were ordered to attend, and no one was allowed to leave during the performances, however pressing the reason. We read of women in the audience giving birth and of men growing so bored that they furtively dropped down over a hundred feet from the back wall. Some even shammed death and were carried away for burial.

Like most patrons of the arts, Nero had a healthy respect for actors. He had the leading actor **Paris** executed because he acted better than Nero did.

The two leading actors of ancient Rome were **Roscius** (died 62 B.C.) and his contemporary **Aesopus.**

Comedy flourished in ancient Rome and produced a number of stock characters: a soldier braggart, a miser, a parasite, identical twins, a resourceful slave, and Benny Hill. Roman theatre produced two major comic playwrights:

(1) **Terence** (185–159 B.C.), an African-born slave freed in Rome, who wrote urbane comedies which were appreciated only by the elite. He was supposedly lost at sea.

(2) **Plautus** (254–184 B.C.), a stage carpenter, who wrote plays which were essentially the first musical comedies, as two thirds of the dialogue was sung.

The Dark Ages

(Not to be confused with the spate of empty theatres in Shaftesbury Avenue a few years ago.) The theatre, like history, vanished at the fall of Rome and did not reappear until the Middle Ages. St. Augustine, once a fanatical theatregoer, forbade good Christians to attend the theatre in case they might enjoy it as much as he had. As a result, actors took to wagons again, and like modern buskers, only the really bad ones had the gall to continue.

Middle-Age Spread

Into the Middle Ages, ragged troupes continued to tour their jugglers, wrestlers, acrobats, dancers, mimics, animal trainers, ballad singers, and raconteurs until each Saturday afternoon at the marketplace was more like Sunday night at the London Palladium.

Then the Church stepped in with a neat U-turn. A nun from Gandersheim with the unlikely name of **Hrotswitha** adapted the plays of Terence and became

the leading playwright of the Middle Ages as well as the first woman playwright.

Then the English church, with the help of the **town guilds,** took Bible stories and made them into play **cycles**, which are popularly known as **mysteries** and **miracles.** It is a mystery why anyone wanted to see them in the first place and a miracle that they were successfully revived by the National Theatre in the 1980s.

Meanwhile, over in Italy, more actors on wagons were inventing **commedia dell'arte,** unbearably loud and raucous improvised plays with nauseating characters like Harlequin, Columbine, Pierrot, and Punch, who rushed around hitting everybody with a two-pronged stick known as a **slapstick.** A few actors today claim to be experts in commedia dell'arte. Have no doubt about it, these are desperate men.

The Age of Shakespeare

In 1572, a Parliamentary Ordinance declared that actors were henceforth to be classified as **rogues** and **vagabonds,** and at last the English tradition of great acting was legally acknowledged.

Four years later, **James Burbage** built the first permanent theatre in London. He gave it the astonishing name of the Theatre. His example was followed shortly by the builders of the Curtain, the Swan, the Rose, and finally the Globe, which was built by his sons, **Richard** (the first great English actor) and **Cuthbert** (who was Richard's manager, and therefore possibly the first **agent**), from the timber of the original Theatre.

Christopher Marlowe was the first English playwright to bring plays up to the level of great literature. The atheist son of a shoemaker, Marlow made a mistake frequently made by modern playwrights – while drinking in a pub in Deptford, he queried the bill and was stabbed to death.

Of the life of **William Shakespeare**, we have about five facts, which include the fact that he was born and the fact that he died. This skimpy biography has not prevented him from becoming the most frequently written about person in history. The pride and joy of the English Tourist Board, the theatrical potential of Shakespeare's work inspired Adolf Hitler to make the pertinent observation that in no country in the world is Shakespeare so badly played as in England.

Shakespeare's friend and contemporary **Ben Jonson**, influenced by the Roman commentator **Horace**, insisted on a five-act structure, which was taken up by all his contemporaries. He wrote some sprightly **comedies of humor.** The Humors bore no relation to anything which might make a person laugh but were part of a medical system in which fluids were thought to govern human nature: the sanguine man was governed by blood, the choleric by bile, the melancholic by black bile, and the phlegmatic by a substance readily available on London pavements. Jonson was accorded the honor of being buried in Westminster Abbey. However, in order not to take up too much space, he was buried standing up. (Recent excavations at Westminster Abbey show that the gravediggers made a small mistake, and in fact Ben Jonson was buried upside down.)

Jacobean playwrights wrote in combinations. Take two or three names from the following list, shuffle them at random, and if the result sounds like a real-estate agent, you can be sure that a play was the outcome: **Beaumont and Fletcher and Massinger and Heywood and Chapman and Shirley and Dekker and Heywood and Marston and Middleton and Rowley and Heywood and Tourneur.** The most famous duo, Beaumont and Fletcher, wrote regularly in tandem until Beaumont did the dirty on Fletcher and got married to someone else. Fletcher then teamed up with Massinger, and the relationship became so close that they were eventually buried in the same grave.

On the accession of James I in 1603, the playwrights, kowtowing to the taste of their new monarch (a man who, incidentally, couldn't fit his tongue in his mouth), larded their plays with ghosts, witches, magic, and masques. And these elements are prominent in the works of the Jacobeans, led by **John Webster,** of whom practically nothing is known.

Commonwealth Capers

Thus British theatre flourished until the rise of the **Puritans.** Realizing that certain things were enjoyed by the people of Britain, the Puritans banned them. These things included maypoles, hot cross buns, dancing, mince pies, horse racing, Christmas day, and the theatre; in short they banned fun.

Meanwhile, of course, theatre in Europe flourished, although it must be said that to the British theatregoer, knowledge of anything foreign need be only slight. Spain produced **Lope de Vega,** a contemporary of Shakespeare's, who wrote 2000 plays, **Cervantes,** who is more famous for the creation of *Don Quixote*, and **Calderon.** France provided the two neoclassical playwrights **Corneille** and **Racine** and the great comic playwright and actor **Molière.**

Restoration Romps

In 1660, the British public, sick of eighteen years of quiet family life, welcomed Charles II, the dashing son of the beheaded Charles I, back to rule. Charles had enjoyed his stay in France, with its glittering theatrical tradition, so shortly after his accession to the throne, he reestablished theatre in London, and with his brother James, he provided financial as well as moral support.

The new theatres were indoors and more like today's Shaftesbury Avenue buildings, but much smaller. The actors acted upon an **apron** stage, and the **proscenium** arch was where it was meant to be—in front of the scenery. Brilliant trick-perspective sets were sometimes embellished by using dwarves and children in grownups' clothes behind the proscenium to establish depth.

The King's most welcome innovation was the introduction of the **actress.** Until then, all female roles had been played by boys. The most famous of the first generation of actresses, **Nell Gwyn,** eventually retired to become Charles's mistress.

The first Poet Laureate, **John Dryden,** wrote far too much, most of it too clever by half. His forte was **heroic** tragedy, bombastic plays in rhyme. He was imitated by **Nathaniel Lee** who, not surprisingly, went mad and **John Dennis,** who stood up in the middle of a rival production's storm sound effects and gave us the phrase "They've stolen my thunder."

The **comedy of manners** was the order of the day and was provided by **William Wycherley,** who went under the nickname "Manly"; the diplomat **Sir George Etherege; George Farquhar,** an Irish actor, who fought in the Battle of the Boyne before stabbing someone onstage and retiring to a career as a writer (he died broke while London rocked with the success of his last play, *The Beaux Stratagem*); and **John Vanbrugh,** better known as the set designer for Granada TV's *Brideshead Revisted.*

The master of the form was **William Congreve,** who is responsible for the quotations "Hell hath no fury like a woman scorned" and "Music hath charms to soothe a savage breast." He retired from playwriting in 1700 and died in 1729 as a result of a coach accident. He left most of his money to the second Duchess of Marlborough, who used it to build a life-size working dummy of him, which sat with her at table and is said to have been able to drink, speak, and laugh at her jokes.

The first English professional woman writer made her debut in the person of **Aphra Behn,** who earlier had been a spy in the Dutch wars. Apart from writing plays, novels, translations, and poems, she also introduced **Thomas Otway** to the theatre by getting him a part in one of her plays. During his first performance, he took one look at the audience and decided to be a playwright. He started the vogue for **domestic** tragedy and was himself a bit of one. After Otway had not eaten for some days, a friend is said to have bought him a sandwich, which he ate so greedily that he choked to death.

Shakespeare was given an airing but was thought too barbarous, so *Macbeth*'s witches sang Italian opera, new characters joined the cast of *The Tempest,* Romeo and Juliet lived happily ever after, as did King Lear and Cordelia, who married Edgar, and Richard III was given a new line which seems to have stuck: "Off with his head . . . So much for Buckingham."

So much for the Restoration.

Middle-Class Mediocrity

The year 1700 was a turning point in theatrical history. Congreve retired, Dryden died, and the ascendant middle classes started their conversion of the British people into respectable, home-loving prudes. The theatre was the first thing to suffer.

To the dismay of everyone with even half a wit, **Colley Cibber,** a slimy snob and social climber, became Poet Laureate, and his gutless **sentimental** comedies led the way. The current tragedy form was true to its name, **bourgeois.**

The leading comic dramatist of the early century was **Susannah Centlivre,** who, as an actress, had specialized in the role of Alexander the Great. Most of her plays, like so many modern comedies, depend on people being stuck in cupboards and behind screens.

The essayists **Addison** and **Steele,** infinitely more successful in their *Tatler* and *Spectator,* provided a few plays, as did **Henry Fielding,** before the 1737 Licensing Act drove him to write novels.

The Licensing Act, which introduced censorship to

the British theatre, was brought in by a government which realized the potential power of the theatre over public opinion. One of the plays which led to its enforcement was **John Gay**'s *The Beggar's Opera.* Produced by **John Rich,** it was said to have made Gay rich and Rich gay.

The notorious Rich family had been involved in theatre management for some time and were responsible for (among other destructive "improvements") shortening the forestage and pushing the actors behind the proscenium in order to cram in more seats and raise profit levels.

Interesting side-effects of the Licensing Act were the lengths to which people were driven to evade it. As only the two Royal theatres in London were licensed to produce straight plays, other ingenious companies were driven to advertise (for instance) a concert, during the interval of which was performed, free gratis, the tragedy of *Othello.* Some did productions of plays where every twelfth word was sung and called them operas; and as they could not legally charge for tickets to straight plays, some managers charged exorbitant prices for cups of chocolate, and every cup of chocolate purchased entitled the drinker to a free performance of their play.

Artistically speaking, the midcentury saw reform in the person of actor **David Garrick,** who insisted on a more **naturalistic** approach and put Stratford-upon-Avon on the map by holding a Shakespeare festival there. His last words were "Oh dear!"

His contemporary **Charles Macklin** had three pauses: the moderate, the long, and the grand. When a prompter interrupted his grand pause, he rushed offstage, punched him on the nose, and returned to enthusiastic applause. He made great improvements in theatrical costume so that, for instance, Roman senators no longer wore periwigs. It was during an argument over a wig that Macklin fatally stabbed another actor through the eye with a stick. He was found guilty of manslaughter, but his popularity saved him from a prison sentence. It is not surprising that at this time there were attempts to prohibit actors and their children from Christian burial.

Richard Brinsley Sheridan, an MP who chalked up a record five-and-a-half-hour speech in the House of Commons, became sole owner of the Drury Lane theatre at the ridiculous age of 27. He had no problem getting his plays accepted by his own theatre, thank goodness, for in them he managed successfully to marry comedy of manners and sentimental comedy and to put the standard of British playwriting back on a high level. (For some reason many people think Sheridan wrote Restoration comedies. This is much the same as believing that Harold Pinter writes Victorian melodramas.) In the House of Commons one day, Edmund Burke tried to stage a dramatic moment by throwing a dagger onto the floor of the House and crying, "Such is the weapon which French Jacobins would plunge into the heart of our beloved king!" Sheridan took the wind out of his sails with the retort "The gentleman, I see, has brought his knife with him, but where is his fork?" The night his theatre burned to the ground, he sat drinking next door in the Piazza Coffee House in Covent Garden and when asked what he was doing, replied, "May not a man be allowed to drink a glass of wine at his own fireside?"

Like many a heroine of the day, his last words were "Alas, I am absolutely undone!"

Oliver Goldsmith wrote only two plays, but he had a busy life. He ran away from university, set up as a doctor but attracted no patients, tried to take holy orders but was rejected by the bishop, decided to run away to America but got stuck at Cork, was then given £50 to start a career in law but lost it at the gambling tables, set out to make the Grand Tour but returned so broke he had to pawn his clothes, and eventually became a proofreader to the novelist Samuel Richardson. He then took to literature himself, writing essays, novels, poems, and at last *She Stoops to Conquer,* one of the finest of all British comedies. The success, however, came too late, and he died £2000 in debt.

Wasn't It Romantic?

The winter of 1808–9 saw both major London theatres destroyed by fire. They were rebuilt, but the replacements were a management's dream and an actor and theatregoer's nightmare: huge, tiered monsters with hopeless acoustics and sightlines, and of course, higher ticket prices. The audiences expressed their indignation with the type of violence now seen only when a penny is added to the price of a pint of beer or Crystal Palace play at home to Chelsea.

Acting thrived with the **Kemble** family, led by **John Philip** and his sister, **Sarah Siddons,** and **Edmund Kean,** who started as a stage Cupid. Kean's preparation for tragic roles included eating raw beef for murderers, roast pork for tyrants, and for lovers, boiled mutton.

British tragic playwriting, however, hit an all-time low when the Romantic poets **Shelley, Coleridge, Bryon,** and **Keats** decided that poems divided among twelve characters were plays.

The Romantics in Germany were much more successful. **Johann Wolfgang Goethe,** who was later given a *von* between Christian and surname, was not just a clever playwright. He became Minister of Finance at the age of 25, had an attempt at refuting Newton's theory of light, and made anatomical history with the discovery of the human intermaxillary bone.

His friend **Friedrich von Schiller,** after studying law at military academy, qualified as a surgeon. His play *The Robbers* caused a storm all over Europe, but predictably the English banned it before it got there. Schiller had gone AWOL to attend the first night and was arrested and forbidden henceforward to write anything but medical books. So he ran away and became the leading playwright of the **Sturm und Drang** (storm and stress) movement. He wrote *Don Carlos,* a play twice as long as *Hamlet,* and a couple of plays which make mincemeat of history and geography but are definitely great drama.

Although Goethe and Schiller had an overwhelming influence on world drama, it is quite unnecessary for the British theatregoer to know anything about them but their names.

Victorian Values and Edwardian Excess

As the nineteenth century rolled on, the British poets (Tennyson, Browning, and Swinburne) were still at it and among them had managed to encourage audiences to stay at home by the thousands. Managers tried to counter this highfalutin' drama with theatre for the lowbrow; so in 1879 Matthew Arnold felt free to declare that there was no English theatre — meaning that literary standards had become subservient to showmanship and box-office receipts.

Edmund Kean's son **Charles** understood perfectly the British need for vulgarity and tried to incorporate as much irrelevant spectacle as possible in his productions of classical plays. Later, **Herbert Beerbohm Tree** did *A Midsummer Night's Dream* with real grass and rabbits. (Both Tree and his wife appeared in it, and a contemporary critic complained that you couldn't see the wood for the Trees.) The public, however, was quite happy to have aquadramas, horse races, and Ben Hur's chariot race onstage with no accompanying literary text to clutter up the action. Thus, **melodrama** thrived.

Henry Irving, the first actor to be knighted, excelled in melodrama, and after his rendition of the telling line "The bells! the bells!" peals of approbation rang through the auditorium. It was, however, not the most famous line in Victorian melodrama; the much parodied "Dead! . . . and never called me mother!" takes that title and also the biscuit.

And as in every other century, there were more moves towards **naturalism. Madame Vestris** had initiated the **box set** (three walled rooms with real doors), and **T. W. Robertson**'s seemingly laughable **cup and saucer** dramas played on them and were seen to be a real breakaway from traditional stereotypical caricatures.

Victorian theatre was run by actor-managers. Apart

from the Keans, the Trees, Madame Vestris, and Irving, there were innumerable lesser talented but equally grand actor-managers whose names sound like small towns in Devon.

The end of the century saw the rise and fall of **Oscar Wilde,** master of the brittle epigram. Described by a contemporary as "a Roman emperor carved out of suet," Wilde was imprisoned for gross indecency with other male persons and lived the rest of his life in Paris under the name Sebastian Melmoth.

W. S. Gilbert (full name: William Schwenck Gilbert — now you know why he stuck to his initials) was also rather a good playwright until Sir Arthur Seymour Sullivan persuaded him to become the very model of a modern major lyricist.

While continental Europe produced a string of great stars like **Rachel, Réjane, Helena Modjeska, Eleanora Duse, Thomaso Salvini,** and **Sarah Bernhardt,** British acting hit the pits with the emergence of **Lillie Langtry,** known to some as the Jersey Lily and to the Princess of Wales as the Jersey cow.

Also in continental Europe, playwrights of incalculable influence, such as **Victor Hugo, Alexandre Dumas, Alfred de Musset, Eugene Scribe, Nikolai Gogol, Alexander Ovstrovsky,** and **Ivan Turgenev** were scribbling away unnoticed by the British.

But there was a group of writers who actually did make some impression in England. Among them, **Henrik Ibsen, Anton Chekhov,** and **August Strindberg** — a collective which could be termed the North Sea Depression — not only brought bored, syphilitic misogynists onto the British stage, but also managed to infiltrate the British repertoire with a force unrivaled by any other foreigners. So much so, that the average English production of an Ibsen play is usually set in a well-appointed house in Cheltenham with a fjord in the garden.

The works of **Henrik Ibsen** are so drenched in the spirit of his native Norway that he had to go and live in Rome, Dresden, and Munich to write them.

Anton Chekhov once claimed, "Medicine is my lawful wife and literature is my mistress." His mistress was actually an actress with the unlikely name of Olga Knipper. His most popular play, *The Seagull,* was booed off on its first performance in Moscow. Usually associated with the yawning and sighing of the naturalism movement, Chekhov denied that his work was naturalistic. "The stage is art," he claimed. "Kamskoy has a picture on which the faces are painted beautifully. What would happen if one cut out the nose of one of the faces and substituted a real one for it? The nose would be realistic but the picture would be ruined."

Chekhov's friend **Konstantin Stanislavski,** the director of the **Moscow Art Theatre,** started writing books which one of our leading actresses has described as "handbooks for bad actors." In these books, Stanislavski explains the elements of performance which are understood instinctively by good actors. This is called the **Stanislavski System** (and should not be confused with the American **method,** which is altogether another thing).

Johan August Strindberg, a horrid little man, was a leading light in every *ism* going. At different times, he led the way in naturalism, realism, mysticism, romanticism, and even expressionism. He hated everything to do with the idea of female emancipation and managed to blame all of the ills of the world on women – in particular, his three wives.

Another foreigner, **Richard Wagner,** made less impression on world theatre with his *Ring Cycle* than by putting out the **houselights** and leaving the audience in the dark, where they have been ever since.

Twentieth-Century Blues

Henry Irving's leading lady **Ellen Terry** had an illegitimate son, the director and designer **Edward Gordon Craig,** who brought us squarely into the twentieth century and anticipated today's directors by publicly confessing that he would rather work with puppets than actors.

In the twenties and thirties, British drama had a field day. **George Bernard Shaw** wrote hundreds of highly articulate dramas, **Noel Coward** tossed off a handful of sparkling comedies, and **Terence Rattigan** bumped up British morale with some jolly stiff-upper-lip plays.

There were a great number of dreadful **historical** plays about everyone from Clive of India to the Brontë sisters by way of Abigail Masham, which may not have done much for world literature or factual biography, but provided wonderful vehicles for the great new British actors like **Laurence Olivier, Ralph Richardson, Sybil Thorndike, Edith Evans, John Gielgud, Michael Redgrave, Flora Robson, Peggy Ashcroft,** and **Donald Wolfit,** who has since been eclipsed by his dresser.

World War II seriously disrupted the work of **Bertolt Brecht,** who spent the thirties in Germany trying to create **epic ensemble** theatre. Adolf Hitler beat him to it, and Brecht fled to America, where his work on **political** theatre was upstaged by the McCarthy trials. Poor Brecht fled back to Germany, where he founded the **Berlin Ensemble** and died.

In post-war Britain, the **angry** playwrights, disgusted by plays about verbose middle-class bores in drawing rooms, started writing plays about verbose middle-class bores in kitchens. There were also a few plays, usually by **Samuel Beckett,** set on rubbish heaps. These are incomprehensible to everyone except those people who would have been able to see the emperor's new clothes.

Most recently, plays have become more like dramatizations of the lead column of the *Guardian,* discussing "relevant" subjects like Northern Ireland, unemployment, South Africa, rape, and the problems of lesbian vegetarian night cleaners in Chile.

A reaction against this worthy work has inspired a style of theatre which caters to the lowest common denominator in British taste: shows which demand a lot in the way of prepublicity, little in the way of script, nothing in the way of plot or acting, and a performing set.

A Note on Oriental Expression

Divinely unaffected by everything that was going on anywhere else in the world, the Japanese painted their faces white and invented the all-male **Noh** theatre. The women, feeling left out, counteracted by inventing all-women **Kabuki** theatre. Rather put out by the competition, the men passed a law banning women from appearing anywhere and declared that henceforth Kabuki would also be all male. Which all goes to show that there's no business like Noh business, like no business I know . . . except Kabuki business, that is.

THE CRITICS

How to Decipher Reviews

When the dust jacket of a novel informs you that Miss X is "the new Jane Austen," you instantly know that her book is full of bitchy remarks, and any novel written "in the style of Virginia Woolf" obviously has no plot. Similarly, theatre criticism in the national press can be easily understood once the technical terms used by the modern critic are decoded. Here are some of the critical expressions most frequently encountered:

Accessible – So banal that a child of five would find it simplistic.

Alienation effect – A device which jars the audience into the uncomfortable awareness that they *are* the audience (for example, the price of their tickets). (Note: This device is sometimes called by its original German name, **Verfremdungseffekt** – a word perhaps Brecht can pronounce, as he seems to be the one who best understood it.)

Avant garde – Even the critic couldn't make head or tail of it.

Black comedy – Comedies, the plots of which have less to do with underpants than undertakers.

Brechtian production – The company couldn't afford a set.

Camp – Loud, silly, and more often than not involving a homosexual element of which the critic thoroughly disapproves and which he dare not openly criticize for fear of seeming antigay.

Comedy of manners – Epigrammatic plays in which nobody ever says what they mean (for example, for the line "Would you like a cup of tea?" read "I would like to rip off your clothes and ravish you now, here on the kitchen table."). These plays can often be recognized by the arch tone employed by the actors appearing in them.

Conflict – Nothing to do with the relationship between director and actors, but the seed of the play itself (for example, Hamlet wishes to kill his uncle but realizes that nice boys don't do such things; to do it or not to do it, that is the conflict).

Delivery – What an actor makes of his lines. Dame Edith Evans's marvelous delivery owed a lot to her dictum – if you don't understand the line say it as though it is improper.

Denouement – The moment when everything that you have understood of the plot so far is proved wrong.

Deus ex machina – From the Greek "God out of a machine." Now means any contrived piece of plot (generally occurring during the denouement).

Dialectical – Packed with dull discussions and analytical arguments.

Didactic – Barrel-thumping, axe-grinding political preaching of the lowest order.

Ensemble – Onstage camaraderie achieved at the cost of much malicious backstage backbiting.

Epic production – A production that is still going on long after the pubs have closed.

Exposition – Scenes generally between a housemaid and an elderly spinster aunt setting up the story so far. For example,

Housemaid: "Times is hard now that Master Giles has had to sell the Bentley and take up basket-weaving to pay us servants' meager wages, and what with Madam being elected chairperson of the Jockey Club, and Miss Prowse now happily married and living in Java, it's fair given me and MacDonald, the new butler, the colleywobbles."

To which the maiden aunt can only reply: "And how is Bill Taylor taking all this?"

Feminist – Productions in which over five percent of the company are women.

Grand Guignol – The type of grotesque overacting practiced mainly by actresses wearing ill-fitting wigs and with lipstick on their teeth.

High comedy – Comedy without any laughs.

Method – An American bastardization of the Stanislavski System of acting; epitomized by James Dean and Marlon Brando and characterized by fumbling gestures, inarticulate mumbling, and torn T-shirts.

Motivation – The driving force behind an actor's line (for example, behind the line "Would you like a cup of tea?" might be the motivation "I really must get rid of these cash-and-carry caterers' teabags.")

Naturalism—The depiction of life at its most boring.

Pinteresque—Scanty, monosyllabic dialogue with pauses you could drive a train through.

Poetic—Long-winded and overwritten.

Polemic—The argument of a play. Sometimes goes like this:

X: Would you like a cup of tea?
Y: No.
X: Oh yes you would.
Y: Oh no I wouldn't.
X: Oh yes you would.
Y: Oh no I wouldn't . . . etc.

Polished—Overrehearsed and smug.

Political—Sympathetic to the Left.

Realism—The depiction of life at its most tawdry.

Song stylists—Performers who can really sell a **number** (song) but who could not *buy* their way into the chorus at La Scala.

Stylish—Adjective used to describe virtuosity combined with confidence and economy. Now used only when describing men in silk dressing gowns.

Technique—Long-forgotton acting art of being heard and finding your light.

Theatre of the Absurd—The theatre's answer to surrealism. In a typical scene a grenadier guard wearing a Las Vegas showgirl's headgear might hand a boa

constrictor to a charwoman (who is quietly whistling Mendelssohn's "Wedding March") with the line "Would you like a cup of tea?"

Theatre of Cruelty—Theatre designed to make the audience suffer. This term can be freely used about most contemporary work.

Vernacular—Anything said to have been "written in the vernacular" is more likely to have been written in the lavatory—copied down from the stuff scrawled on the back of the door.

Well-made play—Overstructured work, the only fault of which is that it is deadly dull.

Working-Class Theatre—Theatre cultivated to instill a sense of well-being and smug superiority in an audience of middle-class, pseudo-intellectuals.

FACT AND FICTION

Time to explode a few theatrical myths and exhibit a few fascinating theatrical facts.

Sarah Bernhardt had a wooden leg.—False.

When Sarah Bernhardt was the grand old age of 72, gangrene set in on the leg which had given her touble all her life. Enroute to the operating theatre, she confidently whistled the "Marseillaise." After a slow recovery she was brought a wooden leg. After a few unsuccessful tries at screwing it on, she screamed and threw in into the fire.

She did not get a replacement and refused to have a wheelchair. Instead she was carried around in a litter and called "Mère La Chaise." The French custom of three knocks to signal curtain-up inspired wags to cry out, "Here she comes!" but even in performance she still refused artificial aids and said, "In case of necessity, I shall have myself strapped to the scenery." In fact, she lay on a couch and at dramatic moments threw herself with superhuman force into the arms of the man playing opposite her. In a typical gesture of Amercian good taste, the manager of P. T. Barnum's touring circus, hearing the news of her unfortunate amputation, telegramed an offer of $10,000 for the offending leg, which he wished to exhibit.

The Mousetrap is the longest running play in the world.—True.

Despite a feeble denouement in which an intelligent and highly articulate detective turns into a raving subhuman imbecile within a matter of seconds, *The Mousetrap* is still regularly putting out the "House Full" notices. The shortest run was probably *The Intimate Revue* of 1930, which didn't even manage to complete its first performance before closing forever.

Many leading playwrights have experienced flops: after the first performance of Noel Coward's *Sirocco,* the audience booed for ten minutes, and then the leading lady, Francis Doble, gave a curtain speech saying it was the happiest night of her life; despite a cast which included Lee Remick and Angela Lansbury, Stephen Sondheim's 1964 musical *Anyone Can Whistle* ran for only eight days; the director of Lionel Bart's *Twang!,* Joan Littlewood, left before the first night of the provincial tryout, and the subsequent London run went with a dull thud; and the combined talents of Andrew Lloyd Webber, Alan Ayckbourne, and P. G. Wodehouse couldn't save their musical *Jeeves* from critical and public indifference.

Some flops were simply asking for it: the Thomas à Becket musical *Thomas and the King* included the song "Will No One Rid Me?"; *Two Cities,* based on Dickens's *Tale of* . . . had Madame Defarge singing "The Knitting Song"; and the Henry VIII musical *Kings and Clowns* gave Henry the song "Get Rid of Her!" (Presumably it was reprised five times.)

"Bloody" was the first swear word to be heard on the English stage.—False.

Before the 1737 Licensing Act, no one knows what people got away with. Certainly many words in Shakespeare are much more dubious that Shaw's use of *bloody.* During a Restoration production, an actress got into a bit of a fluster and omitted the *o* from the word *Count* in the line "Oh my dear Count!" which "put the house into such a laughter that London Bridge at low water was silence to it."

The Lord Chamberlain eventually legalized the word *bloody* in Shaw's *Pygmalion* in 1912, but there was such a furor that it was not heard on stage again until Noel Coward's 1936 playlet *Red Peppers.* More interesting than the words allowed by the Lord Chamberlain's office were the words refused. Examples include replacing the words *shit* with *it, balls* with *testicles, crap* with *jazz, postcoital* with *late evening, piss off, piss off, piss off* with *shut your streaming gob, wind from a duck's behind* with *wind from Mount Zion,* and *the perversions of the rubber* with *the kreupels and blinges of the rubber* — whatever they may be.

Frank Sinatra was the first performer to employ a claque to cheer him along.— False.

In Paris in 1820, a Monsieur Sauton set up an agency to provide *claqueurs* for any artiste or management who felt that it would help their opening night. He could provide 500 or more professional clappers, applauders, and general enthusiasts per show, divided into the following types:

- *Rieurs,* who would laugh at jokes and puns
- *Pleureurs* (mainly women), who would hold their handkerchiefs to their eyes at the moving parts

- *Chatouilleurs,* employed to keep the audience in good humor
- *Bisseurs,* who cried "bis!" or "encore!" at the curtain
- *Commissaires,* who were to commit the piece to memory and be noisy pointing out the merits of structure, witty lines, etc.

My Fair Lady is so called from the words of the nursery rhyme "London Bridge is falling down, my fair lady."– False.

The Dick-Van-Dyke-Cor-Blimey-Mite school of Americanized Cockney came up with the astonishing notion that this was the way a Londoner might pronounce the name of the London district of Mayfair and that Eliza Doolittle's ambition was therefore to be a Myfair Lady. (Then why not a Myfair Lydy?)

The name has cropped up from time to time on the American musical scene. The 1925 Gershwin musical *Tell Me More* started life as *My Fair Lady,* and his 1926 *Oh Kay!* had been *Miss Mayfair.* Lerner and Loewe's *My Fair Lady* itself emerged as *My Lady Liza* and adolesced as *The Talk of London* before becoming the full-fledged *My Fair Lady* in 1956.

Nell Gwyn was really a whore who sold oranges.– False.

Although Eleanor Gwyn came from a very poor background and spent much of her childhood working in a "bawdy house," the evidence is that she was not herself a prostitute but only poured drinks for the customers. At thirteen, she spent a few weeks selling oranges, and at fourteen, she started her short but very successful acting career.

The Poet Laureate Dryden wrote many challenging roles specifically for her, and she became one of the most popular players for speaking prologues and epilogues, the Restoration equivalent to a spot as a stand-up comic. She left the stage when Lord Buck-hurst made her his mistress (with the proviso that she must give up her career), but he dumped her, and she went back to work two months later. When King Charles, intoxicated by her wit and stage style, made her his official mistress, she retired for good and was by all accounts a good and faithful lover. She bore him sons, who received titles from their father, but she refused all offers of a title for herself. Charles's dying words were "Let not poor Nelly starve." She continued to visit the theatre and became patroness of many promising young talents.

Shakespeare wrote 37 plays. — False.

No one is quite sure how many plays, if any, were written by the famous "Bard of Avon." Plays never included in the Collected Works but sometimes attributed to William Shakespeare include *Sir Thomas More, Edward III, The Two Noble Kinsmen* (on which he is supposed to have collaborated with John Fletcher), and a very dull play indeed called *Edmund Ironside.* It was published as a "lost" Shakespeare play, but computer analysis immediately proved that it was, in fact, the work of Richard Green, his arch rival, who referred to Shakespeare as that "upstart crow."

Some people doubt that Shakespeare the player wrote any plays. Some think he might have written the poorer stuff and acted as a fence for someone unable to present himself as a playwright. The main contenders for authorship of the Shakespeare canon include Sir Francis Bacon (the Lord Chancellor), Christopher Marlowe (the playwright), Edward de Vere, 17th Earl of Oxford (court wit and scholar), Sir Walter Raleigh (the soldier and traveler who brought Great Britain tobacco and potatoes), Michel Angelo Florio (a defrocked monk, tutor to Lady Jane Grey), and Anne Whately (a lame nun).

It is traditional for men to play women's roles but not vice versa.— False.

Until this century **drag** roles for men (because their costumes dragged on the floor) were probably seen less frequently than **breeches** parts for women (obvious reason), and not only at Panto time. Recent times have thrown up all-male *As You Like It*s, *Oresteia*s, *Julius Caesar*s, *Antony and Cleopatra*s, male Helens of Troy and Ladies Macbeth and Bracknell, and a disastrous cross-cast *Troilus and Cressida*. The only male role which seems to have maintained its female tradition is Hamlet. In the eighteenth and nineteenth centuries many actresses specialized in breeches roles. The popularity of this tradition is thought by some to be based on the desire of men to see women's legs. However, this theory does not explain away the fact that audiences in general consist of more women than men or that most all-female castings of plays were done at the request of groups of upper-class women.

Among the parts often played by women in the past were Alexander the Great in Lee's *The Rival Queens,* Macheath in Gay's *The Beggar's Opera,* George Barnwell in Lillo's *The London Merchant,* Lord Foppington in Vanbrugh's *The Relapse,* Sir Harry Wildair in Farquhar's *The Constant Couple*, Bayes in Buckingham's *The Rehearsal*, Roderigo in *Othello*, Cardinal Wolsey in *Henry V*, and the title roles in De Musset's *Lorenzaccio* and Rostand's *L'Aiglon*. Plays which have received the all-female treatment include Beaumont and Fletcher's *Philaster*, Killigrew's *The Parson's Wedding*, Settle's *Pastor Fido*, Dryden's *Secret Love*, and Congreve's *Love for Love*.

Abraham Lincoln was assassinated by an actor.— True.

John Wilkes Booth shot the American president during a performance of *Our American Cousin* at the Ford Theatre in Washington in 1865. Undoubtedly, Lincoln would have lived only a few months more even if he had not been shot, because he was suffering from a still incurable congenital disease. *But-apart-from-that,-what-did-you-think-of-the-play,-Mrs.-Lincoln?* jokes have kept the story in the popular imagination.

Actors' good deeds are not so well remembered. In London alone, three institutions owe their very being to the generosity of actors: Burbage's chief rival, Edward Alleyn, the star of Marlowe's tragedies, found and endowed Dulwich College; the annual boat race from London Bridge to Chelsea was started, and prize awarded, by the Restoration actor Thomas Dogget, who also gave it his name — Dogget's Coat and Badge; and apocryphal evidence points to Nell Gwyn being the founder of Chelsea Hospital, home of the Chelsea Pensioners and the annual flower show.

Big Ben is a clock.— False.

Big Ben is actually the bell housed behind the clock in the Victorian Houses of Parliament. Before 1856, when it was overshadowed by this national monument, the expression "Big Ben" was a theatrical term meaning a good or bumping benefit performance. The profits from such a performance went to the specific actor on whose behalf the benefit was held. And so a Big Ben provided actors with a nice supplement to their weekly wage.

QUOTABLE QUOTES

Here are some quotations which it might be worth learning so that you can toss them out with carefree aplomb whenever the situation might present itself. They will be equally at home as interval chit-chat or as conversation fillers when dining out with professionals.

"The only way to see the value of a play is to see it acted." *Voltaire*

"Visiting the theatre leads to fornication, intemperance, and every kind of impurity." *St. John Chrysostom*

"This writing of plays is a great matter." *G. B. Shaw*

"How hard a thing 'twould be to please you all." *Congreve*

"Plays and playhouses came originally from the devil himself." *William Prynne*

"The weasel under the cocktail cabinet." (describing what his own plays are about) *Harold Pinter*

"The most insipid, ridiculous play that I ever saw in my life." (on *A Midsummer Night's Dream*) *Samuel Pepys*

"Gay, trifling, and directly opposite to the spirit of industry and close application to business." (on theatrical entertainment) *John Wesley*

"I divide all productions into two categories: those I like and those I don't like." *Anton Chekhov*

"People don't do such things!" *Henrik Ibsen*

CHOOSING WHAT TO SEE

Of course all would-be theatrical bluffers must put themselves through the chore of occasionally going to the theatre. Reading books about this subject can never be enough. On opening your daily newspaper at the entertainment column, you will be bombarded by hundreds of plays that will "run and run," musicals which will make you want to "jump up and sing," comedies that will have you "rolling in the aisles," and thrillers which will have you on the "edge of your seat," which is all a bit disturbing when you also take into consideration how much that seat is going to cost you. So here are a few rules that can help you make sure your money is well spent:

(1) Don't bother with **smash hits.** You will see so many excerpts on television and read so many interviews with the director, actors, designer, producer, writer, backers, and usherettes that you will know not only the plot and most of the dialogue, but also the color of the leading lady's knickers and where the choreographer goes on holiday. And more's the pity, so will everyone else who speaks English and lives this side of the equator. As a result, any contribution you can make to discussions on the subject of this production can undoubtedly be topped by someone who *really* knows what's going on.

(2) If you insist on visiting a **classic** and are thinking of bringing up the subject in public, do make sure you read at least a synopsis of the play before you get there. This minor preparation will give you a sound basis should you wish to comment on the idiocy of cutting such and such a character and the inspired novelty of setting *Hamlet, Prince of Denmark* in contemporary Los Angeles. It will also give you the confidence to dismiss (with raised eyebrows and a sneer) the designer's coup of dressing all the characters in dungarees and dunce caps.

(3) Get your skates on and rush to anything which "must close Saturday," particularly if it opened only last Monday. The main advantage of witnessing short-run **flops** is that you're bound to be one of only a couple of hundred who do — and most of those will be the family of the cast. These delightful gems of theatregoing will give you miles of dinner-table chit-chat and quite possibly a good laugh in the bargain.

(4) See every visiting **foreign company** (particularly the lesser-known ones) for most of the reasons cited in rule 3 above. Replace only the last sentence: it will give you miles of dinner-table chit-chat and quite possibly a wonderful night out in the bargain.

(5) Avoid **previews,** except as novelty viewing. As most directors do (quite rightly) use them as public tryouts, you could easily find yourself discussing the ludicrous use of live pigeons in the opening scene or the absurd curtain line to the

second act, only to find that they had been cut before the first night. You will thereby expose yourself as a cheapskate (preview tickets are slightly cheaper) and a bit of a vulture (most professionals would prefer their work to be judged only after the official first night).

(6) **First nights** are always worth a try. It's better to get in first if it's a hit, and if it's dreadful, there are usually lots of interesting people in the audience to gawp at when the going gets tough.

(7) Keep an eye out for actors who don't seem to have been hailed by the critics and follow their careers. Acting as **talent scout** is always fun, and if you're bright enough, you could spot someone who does actually become *someone.* This will give you a valuable line in *Didn't-I-always-say-they-were-marvelous?* conversations, which can be filled out with "I'll never forget her rendition of the French maid in *The Whore . . . the Merrier!* at Skegness Rep before it become an ice rink."

THE AUTHOR

The repertoire of world drama as experienced by the author:

Ancient Greece: The chorus of Euripides' *The Phoenician Women.*

Ancient Rome: Nothing. (Well, everyone says they're not meant to be performed.)

Miracles and Mysteries: Mercifully avoided so far.

Age of Shakespeare: Played Hippolyta in Fletcher and Massinger's *The Custom of the Country* and Isabella in Webster's *The White Devil.*

Restoration: Author of *The Female Wits;* played Mrs Marwood in Congreve's *The Way of the World.*

Early Eighteenth Century: Directed Mrs Centlivre's *Wedlock/Deadlock* and *The Basset Table* and Pergolesi's *La Serva Pardona;* author of a biography of Mrs Manley—*A Woman of No Character;* co-adapter, with Giles Havergal, of Samuel Richardson's *Pamela;* played Brigida in Goldoni's *Country Life* and Lucrezia in his *The Impresario from Smyrna.*

Romantic Drama: Played Queen Elizabeth in Schiller's *Mary Stuart.*

Victorian and Edwardian: Lady Caroline Pontefract in Wilde's *A Woman of No Importance,* Metella in Offenbach's *La Vie Parisienne* (in a translation entitled

French Knickers), Polina in Chekhov's *The Seagull,* and Maid in Ibsen's *Hedda Gabler.*

Twentieth Century: Ruth in Coward's *Blithe Spirit,* Mrs Eynsford Hill in Shaw's *Pygmalion,* Andrée in David MacDonald's adaptation of Proust, *A Waste of Time,* Kadija in Genet's *The Screens,* The Mother in Brecht's *The Mother,* Mrs. Peachum in his *Three-penny Opera,* and various suffering Germans in his *Fears and Miseries of the Third Reich.*

Oriental Theatre: The author is a woman

All this and more has been played, directed, or written by Fidelis Morgan for Glasgow Citizens, the Old Vic, the Royal Court Upstairs, Birmingham Rep, the ICA, the King's Head, the Half Moon, Shared Experience, the Glasgow Tron. festivals in Colmar, Amsterdam, and Turin, world tour with the RSC, television, and radio.